GERONIMO
STILTON

Published by Sweet Cherry Publishing Limited
Unit 36, Vulcan House,
Vulcan Road,
Leicester, LE5 3EF,
United Kingdom

First published in the UK in 2018
2018 edition

ISBN: 978-1-78226-366-1

Text by Geronimo Stilton
Art Director: Iacopo Bruno
Graphic Designer: Laura Dal Maso / theWorldofDOT
Original cover Illustration by Roberto Ronchi and Alessandro Muscillo
Concept of illustration by Roberta Bianchi, produced by Danilo Loizedda and Christian Aliprandi
with assistance from Lara Martinelli and Andrea Benelle
Initial and final page illustrations by Roberto Ronchi and Ennio Bufi MAD5, Studio Parlapà and
Andrea Cavallini. Map illustrations by Andrea Da Rold and Andrea Cavallini
Cover layout and typography by Elena Distefano
Interior layout and typography by Rhiannon Izard, Kellie Jones, Chris Ogle and Amy Wong
Graphics by Chiara Cebraro
© 2014 Edizioni Piemme S.p.A., Palazzo Mondadori – Via Mondadori, 1 – 20090 Segrate
© 2018 English edition, Sweet Cherry Publishing
International Rights © Atlantyca S.p.A. – via Leopardi 8, 20123 Milano, Italy
Translation © 2016 by Atlantyca S.p.A.

Original title: *Allarme… topo in mare!*
Based on an original idea by Elisabetta Dami

www.geronimostilton.com/uk

www.sweetcherrypublishing.com

Printed and bound in Turkey

# Geronimo Stilton

# MOUSE OVERBOARD!

Sweet Cherry
Publishing

# A WHISKER SCORCHER

**HOLEY MELTED CHEESE STICKS**, it was a hot day — a real whisker scorcher! The sun sizzled high over New Mouse City, and there wasn't a hint of a BREEZE. To make things worse, my air conditioner was on the blink.

7

Oops, I almost forgot to introduce myself! My name is Stilton, *Geronimo Stilton*. I run The Rodent's Gazette, the most famouse daily newspaper on Mouse Island. Anyway, that day I was home catching up on my accounting. I was head-over-whiskers excited to see that my newspaper had also become the **best-selling** paper on Mouse Island! Then the phone rang.

At the other end, a familiar voice shrieked in my ear.

**I WILL DESTROY THE RODENT'S GAZETTE!**

"Stilton! You Cheddarhead! I can't believe your newspaper has outsold mine! You'd better watch your tail! I will destroy The Rodent's Gazette!"

It was Sally Ratmousen, editor of **The Daily Rat** – my nemesis! I wanted to tell her not to take my success so personally, but she had already hung up on me.

Sally Ratmousen is the publisher of The Daily Rat and Geronimo's number-one competitor.

I tried to go back to my work, but I was worried about what Sally might do. And the heat was making FONDUE out of my brain!

In a panic, I called the repairmice at MouseFreeze Cooling Company. I had to get my air conditioner fixed! But the MouseFreeze receptionist had bad news.

"With this heatwave, all the repairmice are busy. You'll have to sit tight today!"

**Sit tight?!** I would MELT if I had to wait until tomorrow. So I decided to get a little creative ...

MouseFreeze offices!

## FIRST TRY

**1.** I made myself Cheddar lemonade ...

**2.** ... but it was too cold, and I got an awful stomach ache!

## SECOND TRY

**1.** I took an ice bath ...

**2.** ... but I had to get ou quickly because I w turning into a mousi

# THIRD TRY

**1.** I tied ice lollies to my ears and under my paws ...

**2.** ... but my fur got all sticky and attracted fruit flies!

# FOURTH TRY

**2.** ... but I slipped and ended up inside Hannibal's fish bowl!

**1.** I decided to take a cold shower...

After all of that, I finally remembered that I still had an old fan in the attic. It was my last hope for staying **COOL!**

But ... where had I put the key? Was it hanging in the hall? Did I put it in my desk drawer? Was it in the kitchen? Or had I hidden it inside a vase in the living room?

I looked everywhere until I finally found it — still inside the attic door's keyhole! I went in and started to look for the fan. But I quickly got distracted. The attic was full of mementos from my many **ADVENTURES**.

I spotted the cowboy hat the Red Bandit had given to me, and the uniform I had worn when I won the Karate World Championship!

**SO MANY MARVEMOUSE MEMORIES!**

That's where the key is!

13

**1.** The golf clubs I used when I won the Super Mouse Cup with Grandfather William.

**2.** The wetsuit I wore while scuba-diving off Shell Island.

**3.** The old suitcase I used while holidaying at the Ratty Tatty Hotel.

**4.** The skis I used while skiing on Frozen Fur Peak.

**5.** The basketball signed by Bounce Ballmouse.

**6.** The football boots I wore when I won the Mouse Island football tournament.

**7.** The cowboy hat the Red Bandit gave me.

# MY ATTIC

**8.** The chef's hat I wore during the Super Chef Contest.

**9.** The uniform I wore during the Karate World Championship.

**10.** My favourite furry snow boots.

**11.** The astronaut suit I wore during my space mission.

**12.** The crystal gondola Petunia Pretty Paws bought me, which led to my adventure in Venice.

**13.** My great-grandmother Ratricia's collection of chamber pots.

**14.** The fan Thea gave me.

# Achoo! Achoo! Achoo! Achoo!

With a start, I remembered the whole reason I had come to the attic – the fan! There it was high up on a far shelf, right above my great-grandmother's chamber pot collection!

The chamber pots were all colours, shapes, and sizes. Some had designs of different kinds of cheeses; some were made of crystal; some were shaped like Greek columns; others were hand-painted. There was even one in the shape of a cat's head ...

I reached out my paw to get the fan and disturbed a huge cloud of dust.

I sneezed so much, I lost my balance and crashed to the floor. "ACHOO! ACHOO! ACHOO! ACHOO! ACHOO! ACHOO!"

Even worse, I ended up pulling everything on the shelves down with me, including the chamber pots!

CRASH! BANG! SMASH! BANG! BOOM!

With a final crash, the massive chamber pot shaped like a cat's head fell right on top of me. **CHEESE NIBLETS!** That made me see a billion stars – and all their planets!

What a headache!

Rubbing my head, I took the fan down to the living room. Then I sat on my favourite pawchair with an ice pack on my head and the fan blowing at full speed.

17

Ahh, what a relief! I was finally comfortable.

I had almost dozed off when the doorbell rang, jolting me awake.

**DING-DONG! DIIIIING-DONG! DING-DOOOOONG!**

Who could it be? Curious, I hightailed it to open the door.

Ahh, much better!

# GRAAAANDSON!

As soon as I opened the door, I was overwhelmed by a booming yell.

**"GRAAAANDSON!"**

Mouldy mozzarella! It was my grandfather William Shortpaws! I didn't have a chance to ask why he was here, because he immediately roared, "Grandson! What are you doing cooped up in the house with the shades down? Snoring away the afternoon in your pawchair, I'll bet!"

"Actually, with this heatwave, I can't seem to concentrate. And my air conditioner is broken, so —"

HUH???

I tried to explain, but Grandfather interrupted.

"I don't want to hear any excuses! Since it seems like you have nothing to do here, you won't mind that I'm sending you to Portugal! A friend of mine needs a favour, and you're the best mouse for the job."

"Me? Go to Portugal? When? How? And, most importantly, *why*?"

"No questions!" my grandfather snapped. "Hop in the van and get going!"

Only then did I notice there was a minivan parked in front of my house.

The van was overloaded with every kind of baggage. There was even a **HUGE** inflatable duck float!

My sister Thea; Trap, my cousin; Benjamin, my nephew; and his friend Bugsy Wugsy were all ready and waiting for me.

"Are you all going to Portugal with me?" I asked.

"You bet we are, Cuz!" Trap said.

"I can't go to Portugal now!" I protested. "I'm very busy with The Rodent's Gazette!" I wanted to stick around and see what kind of revenge Sally Ratmousen might be plotting.

"No excuses, Grandson!" my grandfather thundered. "I'll take care of the newspaper for you while you're gone."

"You seem a little down," Thea said. "You have bags under your eyes, and your fur is faded. You're too **STRESSED!** You have to come with us. It'll be good for you!"

You look stressed!

I was about to refuse, but Bugsy took my right paw, and Benjamin took my left one. They looked

ARGH!

22

up at me with big, wide eyes.

"Come with us to Portugal! **We'll have a blast!**" they said.

How could I refuse them? "Oh, all right. But I have to pack and –"

I didn't even have time to finish my sentence before everybody pushed me into the van, shouting, **"Yaaaay! We're off to Portugal!"**

I looked out of the window to say goodbye

to Grandfather and saw Aunt Sweetfur and Uncle Greyfur. Aunt Sweetfur looked worried as she waved her handkerchief at me. She dried a tear and called, **"Take care, my little nephew."**

She always worries when we go on trips. But this time, she seemed more anxious than usual! Uncle Greyfur waved goodbye. "Once you're on board, make us proud, Nephew!"

# How Strange!

Why was Aunt Sweetfur so worried about me this time? Why did Uncle Greyfur tell me to make them proud "on board"? Why did Grandfather need me to help someone in Portugal?

"What are we doing in Portugal?" I asked suspiciously.

Thea smiled at me. "We've all been officially invited to Lisbon, Portugal, for a very **important** historic commemoration," she said. "It turns out that we Stiltons are the descendants of a famouse Portuguese rodent!"

Then she glanced at Trap, and he CHUCKLED to himself.

"What exactly will I be doing at this historic commemoration? Who is the friend of Grandfather's

Hee, hee!

who needs a favour?" I asked.

"I don't want to say too much and spoil the surprise," Thea said. "But you'll be doing what our ancestor became famouse for."

Thea and Trap exchanged a look. Trap chuckled again.

*Why all the mystery?* I wondered.

I didn't have much time to think more about it, because Bugsy Wugsy shouted in my ear, "Mr G! We're at the airport! Lisbon is waiting for us!"

Thea checked her watch. **"CHEESE AND CRACKERS!** We're late! We have to hurry, or we'll miss our flight!"

I trudged into the airport loaded down with the

baggage. I wondered who our Portuguese ancestor would turn out to be. Was it a famouse writer? Or a scientist? Or maybe an inventor?

Argh!

I kept thinking about it the whole time we were waiting for our plane and while we were boarding. I was so immersed in my thoughts that I tripped over my own paws and **sprawled** in the aisle!

Baggage flew in all directions, and the inflatable duck float wound up around an old rodent's neck!

All the passengers burst out laughing.

"*HA, HA, HA!*"

"Hey, isn't that Geronimo Stilton?"

"I didn't know he was such a klutz!"

"How embarrassing for him!"

**Squeeeeak! Poor me!**

27

The old rodent with the enormous inflatable duck around her neck frowned at me. **"You should be more careful!"** she scolded.

My fur turned pink with embarrassment. I picked up all the baggage and mumbled my apologies. I finally got to my seat and sank deeply into it. To take my mind off things, I picked up the travel guide on Portugal and began to read it.

# DESTINATION: PORTUGAL

**WHERE IS IT?**
Portugal is the westernmost country in mainland Europe. It borders Spain on the north and east, and it stretches into the Atlantic Ocean on the south and west. Portugal has over 1,100 miles of coastline.

**WHAT'S THE WEATHER LIKE?**
Portugal's climate varies depending on the region. It is commonly hotter and drier in the south, where Lisbon is located, and cooler and wetter in the north. The weather is warmest from June to mid-September, which makes summer a nice time to visit.

**DON'T LEAVE HOME WITHOUT ...**
- A pocket dictionary
- Sunscreen
- An umbrella

# PORTUGAL AND NAVIGATION

At the beginning of the 15th Century, Henry the Navigator, son of the king of Portugal, organised many sea expeditions. He hoped to establish new colonies in West Africa and take advantage of the resources found there – particularly gold and sugar – and was involved in founding the Atlantic slave trade.

In 1497, Portuguese navigator Vasco da Gama led the first European expedition to reach southern India by sea.

Da Gama left Lisbon on July 8, 1497, on his flagship, *São Gabriel*, and was accompanied by three other ships: the *São Rafael*, the *Berrio*, and a smaller vessel that carried supplies.

In November, he sailed around the Cape of Good Hope (which had previously been reached by Bartolomeu Dias, another Portuguese explorer). On May 20, 1498, he landed on the south-western coast of India. It was the first time a European ship had ever been there!

# THE GREAT VASCO DA GAMA

While reading the guidebook, I kept wondering who our **famouse** Portuguese ancestor could be. Did we look alike? He was probably a mouse who loved books and had a fear of travelling like me. Maybe he even got seasick just like I do!

I tapped Thea on the shoulder. "Did our famouse ancestor look like me? I bet we have a lot in common."

She burst out laughing. "Not at all! He was bold, courageous, and not afraid of anything."

I tried not to look offended. "So who is it? I HAVE TO KNOW!"

Trap chuckled. "Tell him," he said. "He can't escape now, unless, of course, he jumps out of the plane!"

Thea smiled. "Well, okay. Our famouse ancestor is – the great explorer *Vasco da Gama*!"

SQUEAK!

VASCO DA GAMA
ME! Geronimo Stilton
He was fearless!
I hate to travel!
He discovered a new route to the Indies!
I sometimes have trouble finding my way home!
He was always ready for adventure!
I'm a big 'fraidy mouse!

My whiskers trembled. **"THE GREAT PORTUGUESE NAVIGATOR?"** I shrieked.

Benjamin, who had overheard our conversation, started squeaking with excitement. "Yeah, that's the one! Isn't that **fabumouse**?"

"I don't understand," I muttered, perplexed. "Are you a thousand percent sure that we are Vasco da Gama's descendants? We don't look anything like him!"

Trap pinched my ear playfully. "You're so wrong, Cuz. You look a lot like him. Both of you have two ears! Both of you have a tail and whiskers! You're practically identical! **A real slice off the old cheese block!**"

"That's not true!" I retorted. "I'm the opposite of Vasco da Gama in every way!"

"All of us Stiltons are his descendants," Thea explained. "They just found out! That's why we are invited on this fabumouse re-enactment of his first expedition. All the descendants of those who participated in that landmark voyage will be on the cruise. **Isn't it mousetastic?**" Thea looked thrilled.

35

I became paler than a ball of fresh mozzarella.

"Did you say cruise? You mean we'll be travelling by s-s-sea?" I asked.

"Yes! Isn't it wild? We'll be on an old sailing ship, just like the one Vasco da Gama used!" squeaked Bugsy Wugsy, full of excitement.

Thea handed me an ivory-coloured envelope. "This is the official invitation. You'll be the guest of honour."

I opened the envelope with trembling paws and read the letter.

**HOLEY CHEESE!** There it was. The letter said that I, Geronimo Stilton, was not only one of Vasco da Gama's descendants but that I had to take on his role in the re-enactment!

**"No way!"** I cried in exasperation. "I get seasick. Besides, I don't even know how to steer a rowboat, so how am I supposed to play Vasco da Gama? Your brain must have as many holes as a slice of Swiss if you think I'm going to board an ancient ship and run the risk of being shipwrecked! As soon as we land, I'm getting on the next flight home!"

I'M SEASICK!

Trap pinched my ear again. "Not possible, Cuz! You can't go back. But don't worry. I brought this inflatable duck in case we get **SHIPWRECKED**."

"Look, Geronimo, I'm sorry, but you can't refuse," Thea said firmly. She leaned in close. "The tourism secretary is an old friend of Grandfather's," she whispered. "Secretary Rattio thinks there's someone signed up for the re-enactment who isn't who they say they are."

"What's that have to do with me?" I whispered back.

"Grandfather and the secretary want you to unmask the potential saboteur!"

**Mouldy mozzarella! I was stuck!**

# THE VASCO DA GAMA ANNIVERSARY CRUISE

Dear Mr. Stilton,

We are honoured to inform you that as a descendant of the great Portuguese navigator Vasco da Gama, you and your family are officially invited to retrace the principal steps of his voyage to India on board the *São Gabriel*, an exact replica of the ship used by Vasco da Gama.

You will have the honour of taking the role of the great navigator and steering the ship yourself. As his descendant, you will certainly understand all there is to know about navigation!

We will eagerly await you in Lisbon on Pier 7 on July 7.

Best wishes,

*Julio Rattio*
Secretary of State for Tourism

# A Slice off the Old Cheese Block

We finally landed in Lisbon. As soon as we got off the plane, a waiting band struck up the national anthem of Mouse Island.

We all placed our right paws over our hearts and sang the anthem together. What a **fabumouse** welcome!

"A thousand voices squeak as one. A thousand tails proudly wag. A thousand whiskers boldly

A thousand tails ...   A thousand tails ...   A thousand tails ...

quiver. A thousand paws raise your yellow flag! Under our fur, a thousand hearts beat for you, sweet, sweet Mouse Island."

Despite my worries about the coming sea voyage, my whiskers trembled with joy at hearing the Mouse Island anthem! We walked towards the secretary for tourism on the **loooong** red carpet rolled out for us. Trap pinched my ear.

"Cousin, I'm warning you. For once, try not to embarrass us –"

But Trap didn't have time to finish his sentence. I was so excited to meet the secretary for tourism, I tripped on the edge of the carpet. ❶ Then I frantically

grasped the air in an attempt to keep my balance, but despite my arm flapping I fell smack on my head! **2** (Luckily, the carpet was soft!) From there, I tumbled into a **mousetacular** somersault ... **3** and found myself back on my paws in front of the secretary! **4**

The secretary applauded with gusto. "Welcome to Portugal, Mr. Stilton! We see immediately that you are a bold, athletic, and courageous rodent — just like your ancestor Vasco da Gama! You are the **SPITTING IMAGE** of him — you're a real slice off the old cheese block!"

I blushed pink from the tip of my tail to the tips of my ears. "Um ... thank you ... but I don't really think I'm anything like Vasco da Gama ..."

Everybody burst out laughing.

No one laughed harder than the secretary. "**HA, HA, HA!** So humble, Mr. Stilton! Just like Vasco da Gama! Like I said, a real slice off the old cheese block."

Trap stepped in before I could say anything else. "You have to excuse my cousin, Mr. Secretary. He's a very modest mouse. Everyone can clearly see that he and our ancestor have a lot in common. They both have

42

# MY ARRIVAL IN LISBON!

1) I was so excited, I tripped on the edge of the rug!

2) I tried to keep my balance, but I fell on my head!

3) I performed a mousetacular somersault ...

4) ... and found myself in front of the secretary!

two ears, two eyes, and one tail!"

**I gave up!** There was nothing I could do. Everyone was convinced I was just like Vasco da Gama! I didn't have time to think any more about it. The secretary invited us to get in a car that was waiting for us at the end of the runway. I shook Secretary Rattio's paw and thanked him for his welcome. I was about to get in when he tapped me on my shoulder.

"Mr. Stilton, I know that besides being Vasco da Gama's descendant, you're also an extremely competent detective. Your grandfather speaks highly of you. As he may have mentioned, I suspect that someone is

Um ... thanks!

CLAP CLAP CLAP

planning to sabotage the São Gabriel voyage! Please find out who it is. You're the only one who can help me!"

As much as I was dreading getting on that boat, I could see the secretary was very worried. He had been so welcoming – I wanted to help him if I could. "You can count on this mouse," I said.

The secretary looked relieved. "The ship will launch tomorrow at dawn," he said. "In the meantime, you can see a little of our beautiful city. Bernardo Almouse, your driver, will be your guide and also your bodyguard. Thank you, Mr. Stilton – and keep your eyes open. **Portugal's honour is in your paws!"**

Keep your eyes open!

You can count on me!

# THIS IS WHAT I CALL MUSIC!

As soon as we got in the car, Bernardo Almouse hit the gas, and we took off. The tyres **SCREECHED** like a scared cat. Then he turned the radio on at full blast. He sighed happily. "This is what I call music! This is fado. It's traditional Portuguese music."

Lulled by the melancholy melodies, I forgot all my worries and became immersed in the *beautiful* sights of the city as they flashed by.

"Are you ready to discover Lisbon?" Bernardo Almouse shouted.

"You're going to love it! We'll visit the Grand Oceanarium, the National Park, and Jerónimos

## FADO

Fado is a famous genre of Portuguese music that became popular in the 1820s and 30s. It was commonly performed in taverns and cafés. The word fado means 'fate' in Portuguese. This type of music is often emotional and deals with heartfelt stories of everyday life.

# BERNARDO ALMOUSE

A mouse of many resources!

He's not just a chauffeur. He's also a tour guide, a bodyguard, and a cook. He specialises in traditional Portuguese dishes made with dried cod. Bernardo is also an extremely talented sailor. He has travelled the seven seas and knows thousands of mysterious legends about the ocean.

He is not afraid of anything or anyone. He's always ready with a joke and is a big talker.

Bernardo's real passion is fado. He listens to it continuously on his car stereo. He even plays the Portuguese guitar and sings fado regularly.

He's secretly in love with the beautiful Maria do Sol, the glamorous and very famous fado singer.

He has fifteen cousins, all of whom are chefs.

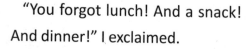

Monastery, and we'll end at the Belém Tower!"

"What an amazing itinerary!" Thea exclaimed.

"awesome!" Benjamin squeaked. "The Oceanarium is one of the biggest aquariums in the world!"

"Bernardo, you didn't mention the most important thing," I said.

"What did I forget?" he asked.

"You forgot lunch! And a snack! And dinner!" I exclaimed.

Bernardo happily twirled his whiskers. "*Nenhum problema!** I have that planned, too! We'll have a picnic lunch at the Park of Nations prepared by my cousin Codmouse the First. Then we'll stop for a snack at the most famouse bakery in Lisbon, where my cousin Codmouse the Second works, and have dinner at Casa de Fado, where my cousin Codmouse the Third works. Then we'll spend the night at the hotel my cousin Codmouse the Fourth owns."

**\* Nenhum problema means "no problem" in Portuguese.**

"How many cousins do you have?" Trap asked, laughing.

"Fifteen! And they're all chefs like my great-uncle, the cook who prepared the best **bacalhau** – salted cod – in all of Lisbon! But enough talking. Here's the Oceanarium! Everybody out. The tour starts now!"

**LISBON:** Lisbon is the capital city of Portugal. The city has a great deal of charm and history. Narrow, steep streets run through its heart. Lisbon lies on the Tagus River and sits on the slopes of several hills. Because of this, there are many breathtaking scenic overlooks.

# BENJAMIN AND BUGSY WUGSY'S NOTES

The Lisbon Oceanarium

Opened in 1998, the Oceanarium is a large aquarium dedicated to marine species that live in the oceans, and to their habitats.

Here we are at the entrance of the Oceanarium. It's truly amazing, mouselets! Uncle Trap was a prankster. (As usual!)

The Oceanarium is home to hundreds of different species of plants and animals. It has over one million visitors each year!

The shark tank was incredible. Too bad Uncle G fainted from fright! (As usual!)

The Park of Nations was the site of the 1998 Lisbon World Exposition, a

world's fair that marked the 500th anniversary of Vasco da Gama's famous expedition. Inside the park, there are shops, restaurants, gardens, and a train station.

The Jerónimos Monastery is located in the Belém district of Lisbon.

It was built by King Manuel I. Many explorers, including Vasco da Gama, stopped here to pray before leaving on expeditions.

Near the monastery is a bakery called Pastéis de Belém, where the specialty is custard tarts, a classic Portuguese treat.

Here's a casa de fado, where popular Portuguese music is played.

# WELCOME ABOARD!

I couldn't enjoy the tour of the city as much as everyone else. The next morning we'd be sailing on a **RICKETY** old ship. **SHIVER MY WHISKERS!** Would we end up stranded on a deserted island? Would we end up as a snack for sharks? I almost fainted from **FRIGHT** when I saw them in the Oceanarium! And to top it all off, someone apparently wanted to sabotage our voyage!

The secretary's words kept popping into my head: *"Keep your eyes open ..."*

Keep my eyes open I did! I was so stressed, I couldn't close my eyes the entire night! Squeak!

The following morning, when Bernardo Almouse took us to the Lisbon port to board the ship, I had bags under both eyes, my whiskers were trembling with stress, and my eyelids kept falling shut. I was even snoring while standing up!

**"ZZZZ! ZZZZ!"**

The secretary stared at me, confused.

"Are you sleeping? I had asked you to keep your eyes open ..."

Always alert, Thea quickly elbowed me in the ribs. "Don't worry, Mr. Secretary. My brother is completely awake ... In fact, I've never seen him more bright-eyed and bushy-tailed!"

57

I tried to open my eyes wider. "Yes, yes, I'm very awake. Look, Secretary Rattio, my eyes are open and ready to spot a saboteur!"

The secretary slapped me so hard on my back that I staggered forwards.

"That's what I like to see, Mr. Stilton. You're awake, brave, and **READY FOR ANYTHING**, just like your ancestor Vasco da Gama! Hurry now, put on the costume. The ship is about to set sail!"

A few minutes later, we were on board the São Gabriel, a replica of Vasco da Gama's famouse flagship.

The ship's entire crew, dressed in period clothes like us, was lined up on the deck of the São Gabriel. We all looked like we had stepped right out of history! Everyone stared at me in complete silence. You could have heard a cheese slice drop. It seemed like the crew was expecting something important to happen – *BUT WHAT?*

I stared back at them, my fur turning pink with embarrassment, not sure what to do.

"Why are they all staring at me?" I whispered to

Thea. "Do I have a pimple on my snout? Do I have **CHEESE CRUMBS** in my whiskers?" I was stumped. Fortunately, right at that moment, I felt someone tap me on my shoulder. I turned and saw a big moustache attached to a familiar smiling face ... It was Bernardo Almouse!

Why are you all staring at me?

"Mr. Stilton," he whispered. "I mean, Admiral! You have to address the crew to start the voyage off on the right paw!"

He handed me a sheet of paper with some pointers for my speech. "It's lucky for you I'm also going on this voyage. Who knows what kind of **trouble** you might get into without me?"

"What are you doing here?" I whispered.

He winked at me. "Didn't you know? I'm also a descendant of someone who participated in Vasco da Gama's expedition. I'm the helmsmouse's great-great-great-great-grandson! The secretary also wanted me to help you track down the potential troublemaker. Better get going with that speech. The crew is getting impatient!"

Trap pinched me on the ear. "Say something, Geronimo. Don't be a **scaredy-mouse**!"

Thea patted my back. "Hurry up and give your speech, Geronimo. The crew is starting to get cranky."

"You can do it, Uncle,"

61

Benjamin exclaimed. "You're representing all of us!"

I quickly looked at the notes Bernardo had handed me. I cleared my throat, stood up straight, squared my shoulders, and tried to look as confident as possible, just like a real admiral would. I gazed out at the crowd. I wondered which mouse out there might be up to no good ...

"Dear rodent friends, welcome aboard the São Gabriel! We've all been granted the **tremendmouse** honour of reliving the experience of Vasco da Gama's first expedition! I hope everyone will do his or her best for the success of this voyage. And now, all mice to their places! Raise the anchor! Set sail!"

DEAR RODENT FRIENDS ...

I turned to Benjamin. "How did I do?" I asked.

"You were **AWESOME**, Uncle G!" he answered.

62

**"Three cheers for Geronimo Stilton, our captain!"** the crew exclaimed.

Within a few minutes, the ship was headed towards the open sea. The water shimmered in the early morning light, and the deck was busy with crewmice.

# THE SHIPS USED BY VASCO DA GAMA

Vasco da Gama took four ships on his expedition: the flagship *São Gabriel*, where he was in command; the *São Rafael*; the *Berrio*; and another, smaller ship that carried supplies. The crew consisted of about 170 men across all four ships.

# MOUSE OVERBOARD!

As soon as we got to the open sea, Bernardo took me to my cabin. He handed me a nautical chart that was exactly like the one used by the great Vasco da Gama.

"Admiral, what's our route? A real captain always knows the best way!"

I squinted at the chart, not sure what I was looking at. I turned it one way and then the other. I flipped it over and then back again.

Which way do I read it?

# VASCO DA GAMA'S ROUTE

Vasco da Gama left Lisbon on July 8, 1497, passed by the Canary Islands, and continued along the coast of Africa to the island of Santiago, Cape Verde. After sailing for several months, he went around the Cape of Good Hope and crossed the Indian Ocean. He landed in southern India on May 20, 1498.

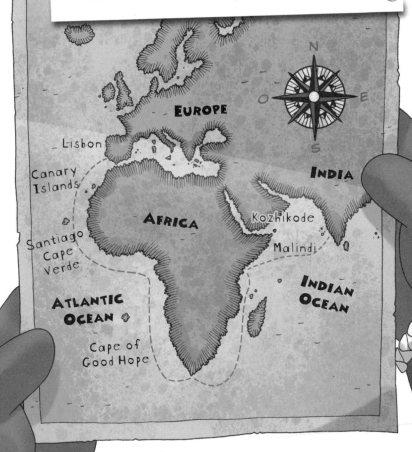

**RANCID RICOTTA!** I couldn't understand one bit of it! Bernardo winked at me.

"A real captain knows seas and currents, sails and ropes, anchors and helms!" he said. "But, between the two of us, I think you're a landlubber and you don't understand any of it!"

"I never said I was a good sailor," I answered, a little offended. "Everybody knows I don't know how to sail, and I get SEASICK!"

Bernardo burst out laughing. "Don't worry! I'll help you get up to speed," he said. "A real captain also knows every single mouse in his crew. Why don't you start by getting to know them? That will give you a chance to see if any of them seem suspicious. I'll take care of the navigating!"

Bernardo handed me a folder with the names and roles of every member of the crew. I rounded up Benjamin and Bugsy Wugsy.

With them at my side, I staggered towards the bridge in an attempt to get to know my crew.

But unfortunately the ship was swaying from side to side. My stomach did **FLIP-FLOPS**, and my snout got warm.

Waves of nausea rolled over me as the ocean waves rolled past the ship. But even though I was getting seasick, I decided to keep going. I didn't want to be embarrassed in front of my crew. And besides, I needed to keep my eyes open for anyone who might want to sabotage our voyage.

# SÃO GABRIEL'S CREW

**GERONIMO STILTON**
Admiral

**BERNARDO ALMOUSE**
Helmsmouse

**GEORGE GORGONZOLA**
First Officer

**MATTHEW MAYO**
On-board Doctor

**PETER TAILWIND**
Sailor

**BRAN ZINO**
Sailor

**MARIO MALGA**
Sailor

**PAULO SAILMOUSE**
Cabin Mouse

**BENJAMIN STILTON**
Student Sailor

**BUGSY WUGSY**
Student Sailor

**TRAP STILTON**
On-board Cook

**THEA STILTON**
Helmsmouse Helper

**1**

UGH!

**MY SEASICKNESS GOT WORSE ...**

Unfortunately, just as I was about to squeak to George Gorgonzola, my SEASICKNESS got even worse.

**2**

**I LOOKED OVER THE SIDE ...**

To hide how **awful** I felt, I looked over the side of the ship to admire the scenery, my fur turning greener than a **MOULDY CHEESE RIND**.

**3**

**AND SOMEONE SHOVED ME!**

"Ah, what a beautiful sea! It's so blue!" Suddenly, I felt two paws on my shoulders. Before I could turn around, someone shoved me overboard! I landed in the water with a giant **SPLASH**!

Fortunately, Benjamin saw what happened. He shouted for help, and an alarm resonated throughout the ship:

**"Mouse overboard!"**

Someone threw me a life ring ... but it landed smack on my head!

**"SQUEAAAK! OUCH!"**

Ouuuuch!

# FISHY FIRST AID

The crew fished me out of the water and rushed me to the infirmary. Dr. Matthew Mayo was waiting for me. He treated the **ENORMOUSE** lump on my head with a compress made of frozen cod.

"Be sure to keep the fish on your injury!" Dr. Mayo said. "It smells a little, but it'll do wonders!"

In fact, it didn't just smell. **It really, really stank!**

As soon as the doctor left the infirmary, Thea, Trap, Benjamin, and Bugsy Wugsy came to see me. They all looked very worried.

"I think someone pushed me!" I said.

"Something **strange** happened to me, too," Trap said. "While I was cooking the fish

for tonight's dinner, someone moved around the food on the stove a second before it would have burned! Who would've done that?"

"That's weird!" Bugsy Wugsy added. "Earlier today, I tried and tried to fold the sails, but I couldn't do it. When I came back later, someone had secretly folded them for me!"

Benjamin nodded. "The same thing happened to me. I

VERY STRANGE!

tried to wind the ropes, but I made a mess of them and got all tangled up. When I went back later to fix them, they were all neatly coiled. Maybe there's a *ghost* on board!"

"There's no ghost," I said, shaking my head. "But Secretary Rattio did warn me to keep my eye out for a mouse who might be trying to **sabotage** the voyage."

Thea shook her head. "But the mysterious rodent Benjamin, Bugsy Wugsy, and Trap described was being helpful. A real saboteur would want to cause as much trouble as possible. I think we're dealing with two different rodents!"

"Well, whoever shoved me in the water wasn't being helpful!" I said, massaging my aching snout. "You might be right. We have to try to catch the saboteur with his paws in the cookie jar!"

"While you rest, I'm going to go with Trap to check

out the kitchen," Thea said. "Maybe I'll find a clue there."

Once everyone left, I fell asleep with the frozen cod compress on my head. I woke up several hours later surrounded by **flies**! The frozen cod had melted, and it was even smellier than before! I quickly washed off and went up on the ship's deck to investigate ... and a **HUGE** seagull swooped down and started to peck me!

I smelled so much like a fish that the seagull thought I was one! Desperate to get away, I jumped into a nearby

lifeboat and hid under the tarp.
The seagull soon flew away.
**Phew!** But just as I was
about to crawl back out,
the lifeboat plummeted
down into the water!

*I'll be safe here!*

Oh no! I would never
survive alone in a lifeboat!

Luckily, I could hear Bernardo Almouse calling for help.

**"Mouse overboard!"** he yelled.

Once they had fished me out of the sea for the
second time, Bernardo pulled me aside. "This was
no accident, Admiral Stilton. Someone cut the rope
securing the lifeboat!"

Someone was definitely up to no good – and it
seemed like they were determined to
**ruin** the voyage by sending me
to the bottom of the ocean!

*EEK!*

78

# THE SABOTEUR!

My whiskers trembled with stress. "It was the saboteur! I'm not safe anywhere!"

"Don't worry, Admiral. I saw everything!" Bernardo grabbed the first officer by the tail. "Here's the saboteur! **It's George Gorgonzola!**"

A second later, Thea and Trap came from the kitchen holding the cabin mouse by the arms.

He won't strike again!

Ah!

It's Paulo, the cabin mouse!

We caught him!

"Here is the saboteur! It's Paulo, the cabin mouse!" Thea shouted.

*"Everybody, stop!"* I exclaimed. "We have one too many saboteurs here! Bring them to my cabin. I'll get to the bottom of this!"

Bernardo took them by the ears and dragged them to my cabin.

"Which one of you is the saboteur?" I asked.

Paulo the cabin mouse burst into tears. To our surprise, he reached up and took off his hair! Then he pulled off a mask! **He was a she!**

"I'm not a saboteur!" she said through her **TEARS**. "I did crash the re-enactment, but I'd never want to ruin it."

I handed her my handkerchief. She dried her tears and continued. "My name is Paulina Pecorina, and I really wanted to be part of this voyage. My great-great-great-great-

THE TRANSFORMATION OF PAULO SAILMOUSE

BEFORE

AFTER

grandfather was Vasco da Gama's personal chef, but his name was never included on the crew list. I didn't get an official re-enactment invitation, so I boarded under a false name and cooked in secret!"

"That's why Trap's been serving such delicious dishes! It's been you the whole time!" Thea exclaimed. "You even kept Trap's fish from burning."

"Give me a little credit!" Trap muttered.

Paulina blushed. "I just love cooking. I'm sorry about all this – but I never sabotaged anyone. **You have to believe me!"**

"I do believe you," I reassured her. "In fact, from now on you'll be the official ship cook!" I said. "I'll let Secretary Rattio know about the error and have him add you to the official voyage participant list."

Paulina dried her tears. "Thank you, Admiral Stilton! That's very generous. I'm going to cook all my great-great-great-great-grandfather's **SECRET** recipes. They're all here in this old recipe book I brought. It's been handed down in my family for generations!"

"That recipe book has to be worth its weight in

# THE STORY OF PAULINA PECORINA, ASPIRING CHEF

Paulina's great-great-great-great-grandfather was Vasco da Gama's personal chef.

But he was never identified in the ship's records, so Paulina joined the re-enactment in secret!

Paulina cooked when no one was watching ...

... until she got caught!

gold!" Trap exclaimed. "We could publish it and become millionaires!"

"Paws down, Trap!" we all shouted together. "The recipe book is secret!"

With one potential saboteur cleared, we had one suspect left. I turned to the first officer, George Gorgonzola. Suddenly he took off his hat, tore off his false whiskers, and removed his mask! What an enormouse surprise! It was none other than my nemesis, **Sally Ratmousen**!

"It's me, Stilton!" Sally snarled. "When I came to your house to continue our conversation, I overheard that you had been invited to Portugal. I followed you here and snuck on board this ship under a false name! I wanted to show everyone what a **fool** you really are!" Sally explained triumphantly. "I took

*My secret recipe book!*

*WOW!*

photos of all your most embarrassing moments! I'm going to do a front-page story all about how ridiculous you are. It will sell out — mark my words! I can just see the headline: NEWSMOUSE DISGRACES FAMOUSE NAVIGATOR! GERONIMO STILTON RUINS RE-ENACTMENT!

"Sales of **The Daily Rat** are going to go up, up, up! And sales of The Rodent's Gazette are going to go down, down, down!"

Before we could stop her, Sally dashed out of my

THE TRANSFORMATION OF GEORGE GORGONZOLA

BEFORE

AFTER

cabin. We chased after her, but she was surprisingly fast! Once on deck, she dove headlong into the sea and then boarded a waiting speedboat.

"You're finished, Stilton!" she yelled as she zoomed away. **"Your Cheddar is shredded!"**

YOUR CHEDDAR IS SHREDDED, STILTON!

# SAY CHEESE!

Now that we knew Sally had been the saboteur, I felt miserable. Not only was it my fault the success of the re-enactment had been put in danger, now Sally was going to publish embarrassing pictures of me!

I began to sob. "When Sally prints those photos, all of New Mouse City will be laughing at me!"

Bernardo Almouse grinned. "Calm down, Admiral. That **cheesebrain** won't be printing anything – because I have her photos!" he said triumphantly. "I took her camera out of her bag while she was talking. **HEE, HEE, HEE!**"

I was so relieved, I gave Bernardo a giant hug! I thanked him from the bottom of my heart and took a peek at Sally's photos.

**HOLEY CHEESE!** They were dreadful!

# SALLY RATMOUSEN'S
# PHOTOS

**PHOTO #1**
Geronimo was always seasick!

**PHOTO #2**
Geronimo's so clumsy, he kept falling in the water!

**PHOTO #3**
He had to be constantly rescued!

**PHOTO #4**
The seagulls even thought he was a fish!

"You're a true friend," I said to Bernardo. "Thank you so much. I don't know what would have happened without you!"

"You would have been the laughing stock of New Mouse City!" Trap said, snickering.

I smiled. "For once, Trap, you're right!" I agreed. I turned around to face the crew, who had gathered behind us. "Dear friends, all's well. We found the saboteur! To celebrate, we'll have a **great big party.**

Hooray!

We found the saboteur!

Paulina will cook all her secret recipes!"

Everyone was thrilled that the troublemaker had been unmasked. **"Three cheers for Admiral Stilton! Hooray! Hooray! Hooray!"** In the moonlight a few hours later, we had a fabumouse banquet on the deck.

# ANOTHER DA GAMA!

The following morning I woke up with a start. I heard a loud noise coming from above.

FLAP! FLAP! FLAP! FLAP! FLAP! FLAP! FLAP! FLAP! FLAP! FLAP! FLAP! FLAP! FLAP! FLAP! FLAP! FLAP! FLAP! FLAP! FLAP! FLAP! FLAP! FLAP! FLAP! FLAP! FLAP!

The noise was getting louder and louder! What could it be? I quickly got dressed and ran out on deck. A gusty wind nearly knocked me head over paws. **DOUBLE-TWISTED RATTAILS!** It was a helicopter!

A few seconds later, Secretary Rattio climbed down from the helicopter. With him was a rodent I didn't recognise, wearing a Vasco da Gama costume just like mine. As soon as they touched the ground, the secretary came over to me.

"Mr. Stilton, I'm so sorry, but we've made a **terrible**

**mistake.** You're actually not a descendant of Vasco da Gama. The real descendant is this gentlemouse, Victor da Gamouse!"

I shook Victor's paw. "Welcome aboard! I can tell right away that you are da Gama's descendant — you look just like him. You're a real slice off the old cheese block!"

The secretary looked embarrassed. "Our historians mixed up the two of you in their report. Mr. Stilton,

Welcome aboard!

NICE TO MEET YOU!

GERONIMO STILTON, PUBLISHER OF THE RODENT'S GAZETTE

VICTOR DA GAMOUSE, EXPERT SEA CAPTAIN

96

you are really a descendant of Luís de Camões. He's famouse for having written *The Lusiads*, an epic poem which tells the story of Vasco da Gama's journey."

I couldn't believe my ears! "I'm the descendant of a FABUMOUSE writer!" I said. "No need to apologise. I'm truly honoured!"

Secretary Rattio cleared his throat. "Therefore, Mr. Stilton, I want to thank you for all you've done so far, especially for exposing the saboteur. But Victor will be taking over the rest of the sea voyage," he said, twisting his paws anxiously.

**"I'm thrilled!"** I exclaimed, relieved. "I can now honestly say that I don't know a thing about ships, sails, or navigation – and I get terribly seasick!"

"In that case," Secretary Rattio said, "how would you feel about spending the rest of your time in Portugal holding a series of lectures on Luís de Camões and his epic poem *The Lusiads*?"

Thea, Trap, Bugsy Wugsy, and Benjamin answered for me, all shouting together. "We accept! When do we leave?"

# Luís de Camões and The Lusiads

**LUÍS DE CAMÕES**
(Born in Lisbon c. 1524, died in Lisbon June 10, 1580)

Luís de Camões is considered Portugal's greatest poet. His most famous work is The Lusiads, an epic poem.

**THE LUSIADS (1572)**
The Lusiads is an epic poem in ten sections that celebrates the history of Portugal, blending reality and myth. The epic also tells the story of Vasco da Gama's voyages and other Portuguese travellers who travelled past the Cape of Good Hope and from there opened up a new route to India.

"Right now, if you want!" the secretary responded. "We could set up a seminar tomorrow morning at the Belém tower."

We said goodbye to the crew and packed up all our things. Half an hour later, we took off in the helicopter. **Destination: Lisbon!**

# There's No Place Like Home!

A week later, once the lectures were finished, we reluctantly left Portugal and returned to Mouse Island. Although I was glad to be back, I missed the beautiful places we had seen and all the new friends we had met: Secretary Rattio, Bernardo Almouse, Paulina Pecorina, and all the crewmice.

**It had been a wonderful trip!**

With a little regret, I unpacked my suitcase. Inside, I found the Vasco da Gama costume I had worn during the São Gabriel's voyage! The secretary must have snuck it into my baggage while we

I missed you, Hannibal!

102

were saying our goodbyes. I carried it up to the attic, where I keep the mementos of my many **ADVENTURES**.

So many memories!

In the suitcase was also an old and valuable edition of the works of Luís de Camões, my famouse ancestor. The books were given to me as a parting gift by the secretary. I took them to my library and placed them carefully on the bookcase, right in front of my desk. There they'd always be close to me, and would remind me of Lisbon and the boat voyage – and of a special piece of my heritage!

I couldn't wait to see what other mementos my future journeys would bring. And I know I'll do my great ancestor proud by writing about every adventure!

**Until next time, dear mouse friends!**

# THE RODENT'S GAZETTE

1. Main entrance
2. Printing presses (where everything is printed)
3. Accounts department
4. Editorial room (where editors, illustrators, and designers work)
5. Geronimo Stilton's office
6. Geronimo's botanical garden

# MAP OF NEW MOUSE CITY

# MAP OF MOUSE ISLAND

1. Big Ice Lake
2. Frozen Fur Peak
3. Slipperyslopes Glacier
4. Coldcreeps Peak
5. Ratzikistan
6. Transratania
7. Mount Vamp
8. Roastedrat Volcano
9. Brimstone Lake
10. Poopedcat Pass
11. Stinko Peak
12. Dark Forest
13. Vain Vampires Valley
14. Goosebumps Gorge
15. The Shadow Line Pass
16. Penny-Pincher Castle
17. Nature Reserve Park
18. Las Ratayas Marinas
19. Fossil Forest
20. Lake Lake
21. Lake Lakelake
22. Lake Lakelakelake
23. Cheddar Crag
24. Cannycat Castle
25. Valley of the Giant Sequoia
26. Cheddar Springs
27. Sulphurous Swamp
28. Old Reliable Geyser
29. Vole Vale
30. Ravingrat Ravine
31. Gnat Marshes
32. Munster Highlands
33. Mousehara Desert
34. Oasis of the Sweaty Camel
35. Cabbagehead Hill
36. Rattytrap Jungle
37. Rio Mosquito
38. Mousefort Beach
39. San Mouscisco
40. Swissville
41. Cheddarton
42. Mouseport
43. New Mouse City
44. Pirate Ship of Cats

## HAVE YOU READ ALL OF GERONIMO'S ADVENTURES?

# ABOUT THE AUTHOR

Born in New Mouse City, Mouse Island, GERONIMO STILTON is Rattus Emeritus of Mousomorphic Literature and of Neo-Ratonic Comparative Philosophy. For the past twenty years, he has been running The Rodent's Gazette, New Mouse City's most widely read daily newspaper.

Stilton was awarded the Ratitzer Prize for his scoops on *The Curse of the Cheese Pyramid* and *The Search for Sunken Treasure*. He has also received the Andersen Prize for Personality of the Year. His works have been published all over the globe.

In his spare time, Mr. Stilton collects antique cheese rinds and plays golf. But what he most enjoys is telling stories to his nephew Benjamin.